My Daily Greetings
Mis Saludos Diarios

Written by
Monica Roman-Tiplin

English - Spanish

Illustrations by
Winda Mulyasari

FROM THE AUTHOR –

Growing up in Bolivia, we are taught very young to always greet our elders especially those who made eye contact which often included people we didn't know.

Good mornings, Good afternoons and Good evenings were always required.

Living in the Washington, D.C. area most of the time we walk by people and a simple quick Hello is shared. Visiting Bolivia I am reminded every time of this custom that everyone follows as part of their everyday life. This is custom and tradition I am teaching my children, so they too will be those walking by greeting others especially their elders.

Creciendo en Bolivia, de muy pequeños nos enseñan a saludar a los mayores especialmente aquellos que nos dan la mirada que muchas veces son personas que no conocemos.

Buenos días, Buenas tardes y Buenas noches eran siempre requeridas.

Viviendo en el área de Washington, D.C. muchas veces cuando pasamos caminado la gente se da un simple y rapido hola. Visitando a Bolivia me recuerda de estas costumbres que todos siguen en sus vidas diarias. Está costumbre y tradición les enseño a mis hijos para que ellos también saluden a la gente al pasar en especial a los mayores.

For my sweet baby boy… mi papito,

Lucas Skyler Tiplin

~ Mama loves you very much

Each morning when
I wake up I greet
my family

Cada mañana al
despertar saludo a
mi familia

Good morning mama!
¡Buenos días mamá!

Good morning daddy!
¡Buenos días papi!

Good morning grandma!
¡Buenos días abuelita!

And I also greet my
doggy everyday

Y también saludo a mi
perrito cada día

I give my family lots of hugs and kisses before leaving home

Le doy a mi familia muchos abrazos y besos antes de salir de casa

In the afternoons I also give lots of greetings

Por las tardes también doy muchos saludos

Good afternoon teachers and friends, bye!
Buenas tardes profesores y amigos, ¡adios!

Good afternoon neighbor!
¡Buenas tardes vecino!

Before going to bed
I say good night to
my family

Antes de ir a dormir
doy las buenas noches
a mi familia

Good night grandma
Buenas noches abuelita

Good night sister
Buenas noches hermana

Good night daddy
Buenas noches papi

Good night mama
Buenas noches mamá

I love you family!
¡Los amo familia!

See you tomorrow

Nos vemos mañana

Made in the USA
Middletown, DE
31 October 2020